ON THAT NIGHT

28,323

ON THAT NIGHT

Elizabeth Yates

Illustrated by James Barkley

E. P. DUTTON & CO., INC.
NEW YORK 1969

Second Printing October 1969

Copyright © 1969 by Elizabeth Yates McGreal
All rights reserved. Printed in the U.S.A.

Published simultaneously in Canada by Clarke, Irwin & Company Limited, Toronto and Vancouver

Library of Congress Catalog Card Number: 70–81984

A23520

For my sister
VIRGINIA YATES ERB
who made Christmas meaningful and
ever memorable.

Each year of our childhood,
she retold the ancient story in a new play
in which we all acted as a gift to our parents
on Christmas Eve.

Contents

ONE

AT THE MANGER

Among the many legends that have to do
with Christmas Eve, there is one that says
on that night lost things are found again.

It was Christmas Eve and the life of the town had
stilled. Stores were closed, people had gone to
their homes, the streets were all but empty. An
earlier snowfall added to the quiet. The night was
dark, except for the stars that now shone bril-
liantly, and the few streetlights; the night was
cold, but windless.

When, from the church near the center of the
town, lights began to bloom, the candles in the
windows held out their welcome. Soon the sound
of organ music came from the church. Carols
long familiar, long loved, played as softly as the
snow had fallen, told of the Candlelight Service
that would soon take place.

People began to appear on the streets, leaving

their houses and walking toward the church; leaving their cars and going up the steps in family groups, or twos, or singly. They were drawn by the light and the music as others had been drawn for years past; drawn by an old, old promise that could fill the eyes with wonder, the heart with amaze.

Against the thrust of the cold, some huddled more deeply into their coats, pushing hands down into pockets; others clasped hands or reached instinctively for a clasp that was no longer there. Up the wide stone steps they went to shove open the heavy door and walk into the church, into the light within. Many candles made the warmth fragrant; the music made it friendly.

People found their places, some in family pews; some, who were in the church for the first time or had returned after an absence of years, went wherever there was an opening. There were those whose joy suffused their faces; there were others who harbored their secret sorrows. But all shared the wonder of the time when, for a space, everything became new, transparent, beneficent. Here, for this hour, all was tender; here, because life was young and heaven-sent, there was hope.

At the front of the church and left of the center aisle, set apart by a railing, was Bethlehem. A few boards had been put together to indicate the side walls and roof of a stable; hay had been spread on the floor and on it a manger had been laid. Two figures were near the manger. Mary was kneeling, her hands across her breast, her gaze on the sleeping Babe; Joseph was standing beside her, his gaze, too, directed into the manger; one hand hung free, the fingers of the other were curled around a staff. In the background, only their heads visible, were the ox and the ass who had withdrawn from their manger that it might serve another purpose.

The figures had been carved many years ago by a craftsman who loved and understood wood. They were plain, uncolored, and beautiful. They had been a part of the church, and so of Christmas, for as long as anyone in the town could remember. On either side of the manger scene stood a candle, the holder high enough to shed light on the faces. Three white chrysanthemums bloomed in their pots just within the railing. The only color was the woven cloth that covered the sleeping Babe. His hands rested on it, crumpled in sleep. It was no single color but a muted medley, as if a garden of flowers had pressed themselves into one small square.

A traditional part of the Candlelight Service was for people to leave their pews and visit the Bethlehem tableau, either before the service commenced or at its conclusion. As the outer door opened and closed to admit more people, as the organ played and the candle flames reached up, those who wished left their places to approach the manger. Some stood in contemplation, others knelt in prayer. Children became quietly wise; older folk surrendered their sophistication.

A little girl who had come into the church with her father and mother left them to walk solemnly down the aisle. For her it was not an aisle but the road to Bethlehem, and the journey was not long. She took each step with expectation. So young herself and close to the miracle of life, she accepted miracles as life, looked for them, recognized them, and welcomed them. When she reached the railing, she stood the better to see and be a part of the scene. Her breath came in quick, little gasps. A smile spread slowly until her whole face was transfigured by it. She was caught up by the moment's marvel: the stable at Bethlehem was inside her church and she was inside the stable.

Since so much had happened already, much more could happen. Her gaze rested on the hay, sure that it would bloom before her eyes as the old stories said it did; she stole a glance at the ox and the ass. Though she could see only their heads, she knew without a doubt that they were kneeling and would soon be talking together. She dropped her eyes to the three pots of chrysanthemums: the Star that had guided the Wise Men had come to earth to bloom in this manner at the entrance to the stable.

She thought of the stories told about this night and of the astonishing things that had happened. Any one of them might happen again, if not at this very hour then later on, or perhaps much later after everyone had gone home and only Bethlehem remained. As she stood there, she had a conversation with the Babe. It was made easier and completely between themselves because he was asleep. In words meant for his ears alone, she told him that she had lost her little wooden horse that was her favorite toy.

"—and I've had him so long, almost since I was as small as you. I take him to bed with me every night because he just fits under my pillow, I take him everywhere with me. Tonight I put him outside on the step to get some air before bringing him to church, then I went back to the house and when I came out again he was gone! I looked and looked, but——" As she came to the end of her story her face wilted and her eyes filled with tears. "Now he is lost, but you can find him for me. Please, little Lord Jesus."

She became silent within as her lips shaped the words of her prayer.

If the horse had suddenly appeared at the manger, she would not have been surprised. It would only have been part of the miracle that was this night. But nothing like that happened. What did happen, and whether it was because her eyes were filled with tears and everything was magnified, was that as she looked at the sleeping Babe she realized that his hands were empty. No toys lay beside him in the hay. Her sorrow for her own plight faded into the sorrow she felt for a baby with nothing to play with when he woke from sleep. She dropped to her knees on the bench that had been placed by the railing. Doing so, she gave up any chance of seeing the face over the rim of the manger.

"When I find my little wooden horse, I'll bring him to you to play with," she whispered.

She got up, turned quickly and went back up the aisle to slip into the pew where her parents were and take her place between them.

He didn't know why he had come or what he was doing there. Church wasn't for him. It hadn't been for many years; perhaps if it had, things might not have gone as they did. But it was cold outside and he had an hour to spare before he was due at the nursing home. He had seen people turning in to the church and he had followed along with them. He felt safe in the assurance that no one would recognize him; he had been gone so long from the town. His hair had grayed, and the beard had quite altered his appearance. Even his mother wouldn't know him, but that would hardly matter now. The last letter that found him had said she remembered only the past; things of the present didn't count with her. "Better come soon," the letter had said.

He didn't know what good it would do. There was no money left even to bury her, though theirs had once been a proud name in the town. All of that was behind him. He had come back and he would see her. They had said they could give him a room at the home so he could spend Christmas with her. "Don't be surprised if she thinks of you as a boy," the letter warned him; "that is the way things are with her now." That was what had appealed to him: he could be the boy he once had been more easily than the man he had become. As if to prove it to himself, here he was doing something that he had not done since he was a boy.

He watched as people left their places, approached the manger scene, lingered briefly, then returned. Better go now, he told himself, before the church fills up and while there's some general movement, less apt to be noticed. It was a long time since he had stood before the manger. He wondered if it would look the same as it had when he was a boy, or if anyone had changed it. Leaving his place, he moved down the aisle with the stealthy gait that had become his stock-in-trade, like a cat, not quickly, not slowly, but boards that could creak under another's tread were silent under his.

His eyes, shifting their glance from right to left, were used to sizing up a thing, a situation, a person; used to looking for an exit or for the move that might be indicative of danger. At a glance he saw it all and it was exactly as it had always been: the figures of the man and the woman, their hands harmless, their eyes on the manger; the two animals standing in the shadow. Why, even the baby hadn't wakened yet! When he had stood by the manger as a boy, it had seemed so real. He had been sure that he could see the Babe breathing, hear the chumping sound an animal makes as it chews its cud. Now he saw them for what they were, wooden figures, plain and drab. Why didn't the baby ever wake up, grow up? Why—then the bearded man felt glad that the baby continued to sleep. He had lost his self-respect so long ago that the reproach in open eyes might have only added to his bitterness.

He could look at the sleeping face and think what it might be like to be young again, to be able to begin life again. He raised his head as if to look straightforward for a fraction of time. As he did so, he didn't know what to do with his hands. They seemed to be in his way. He wasn't going to bring them together in prayer as the woman's were, and he had no broken-down stick to close them around as the man had; so he thrust them deep into the pockets of his overcoat. The right one closed with practiced fingers about the small metal object with which he felt safe; the left one explored that other object he had recently come by.

Once, he had been proud of the things his clever fingers slipped away from their owners—papers, jewels, all with value that could be converted into cash. However, he had nothing to show for any of that now, but the object in his left pocket proved that his eyes had not lost their sharpness and that his fingers were still agile. Turning away from the manger, he walked to the rear of the church in cat steps that were not quick nor slow but quiet.

He found his place in the pew at the rear. He would leave before the service was over and while the last hymn was being sung. He knew where the door was—ten steps would get him to it; his fingers knew how the handle worked, he had tried it when coming in; three steps down, or was it four, and he would be on the short walk that led to the street. As he had been nameless and unnoticed among the people in the church, he would be the nonentity he wished to be once he had left the church. On the seat before him was a woman's handbag. He studied it. It would be a simple matter during one of the hymns to open the bag,

slide out some bills or a wallet, and close it before the hymn was over. He had done it often before and never been caught.

She hurried up the steps and pushed open the heavy door. A quickly drawn gasp of relief caught and tangled with her panting breath. She wasn't late then, but the church was almost full. Her eyes roved from one side to another as she looked for a place to sit. Halfway down the aisle she spied an opening and went toward it. Once settled in a pew, she realized that people were still going up to the front of the church for their visitation to the manger and she thought that she had best do it before the service started. It would take much less time, as most of the people went up after the service. She remembered from previous years that there was always a long queue then and nobody ever seemed in any hurry to get away. If she went now, she could get up ahead of the crowd and be on her way home that much sooner. She nudged the man beside her, then motioned with her lips asking him to save her seat. The man smiled, his eyes partially closed as if he were far away. Nodding, he laid his hand on the seat to indicate that the empty place would be kept.

Leaving the pew, she walked quickly down the aisle, her high heels clicking; but so used was she to the patter of her own gait following her that she was not conscious of the sound. Time was like a dog yapping at her heels, always driving her on. When she reached the manger, the peace of the old tableau arrested her. She stood as still as if an invisible noose had been thrown around her and held her fast.

In her own surprise she stared at the scene that was so familiar and so unchanged from year to year. She wondered why she had come when she knew what it was and what the Candlelight Service would be like. She told herself that it was quite unnecessary to have come when she had so much to do at home. There were presents to be wrapped, there were still cards to be written and mailed. The cards would be late, of course, but that was the way the days were, never enough time to get everything done. Defending herself as she stood by the manger, words raged insistently through her mind.

How could she be expected to hold down a job and run a home and see to the children with what

pieces of time and fragments of energy were left? But if she didn't do it, who would? They couldn't live on just one salary and everyone knew that doctors' bills were the last to be paid. She had suspected before she was married that she would have to carry more than her share in the household. She wouldn't have minded if there were more hours in the day, more minutes in each hour. If she hadn't come tonight, she might have got herself caught up. She thought again of all the things she could be doing if she were home. But it would have been no use. The children would have clamored for her attention and there would have been less chance than ever to do all that had to be done. Well, Roger could get them to bed. He had set the night aside for them and had urged her to go to the service. When she got back, the children would be asleep and she could get on with the business of trimming the tree and wrapping the presents.

She dropped to her knees as the surge of an unfamiliar emotion swept over her : for one perilous moment time was standing still. It always did, at this place, before this scene. That was probably why she had been willing to come. She wanted to be reassured that out of the whole year, out of the pressure of a day, the spending of an hour, there was a moment when time, as such, could not be counted.

She had lost something long ago and she felt fleetingly that she might find it again if she could stay long enough in the odd-remoteness yet close-intimacy of the familiar scene before her. She looked at the Babe, sleeping as if there was all the time in the world for him to do just that; which, of course, there was. She smiled at him almost as if he were real. She wondered what color the eyes of the baby Jesus had been. Dark brown like most Hebrew children? Or gray, the color that seemed to harbor dreams? Abruptly she faced reality. Could she have said what color the eyes of her own children were—the boy, close to ten and so like his father? the girl, close to eight and so totally unlike her mother? Eyes have a way of changing color. She realized how long it had been since she had really looked into the children's to see what dreams were there or, she gave an involuntary shudder, what fears.

The noose slipped from her and she hurried back to the place in the pew that was being saved for her. Her high heels clicked like little casta-nets, in time only with herself and completely out of time with the music that rolled from the organ and wrapped the people in a cloak of comforting sound.

The young man with the thatch of brown hair and squared shoulders had been among the first to enter the church. He had taken off his coat and bunched it into a pillow on the seat beside him. There was nothing to do but sit and wait; in the mood he was in, he didn't care how long he did both. He had just lost his job and the only thing he had to do was find another; but that couldn't be done until the day after tomorrow. He didn't know what he was going to look for, where he was going to go, but it was friendly in the church and it gave him a chance to start thinking things out. They'd been friendly at the factory, too, earlier that day, given him his check and a small Christmas bonus added to it. He hadn't expected that. He'd been at the factory only a couple of months and he knew from the start that he had not done a particularly commendable job.

Ever since he had graduated from college, nearly six months ago now, he had taken what work he could find, forcing himself into a mold as he forced parts on an assembly line, telling himself that as soon as he made some money, got married, got established, he would do the work he really wanted to do; but the hope was like a horizon that kept receding before him.

He had been to Christmas Eve services in other communities, but this was the first time he had ever been to one where people went to the manger scene to view it, or pay their respects, or whatever the reason. Ever since the first person had gone down the aisle, he had been watching them all, wondering what drew them, what they were thinking about, what it meant to each one. Wondering, he built in his mind a story about each one, then the stories began to interweave like the threads of a tapestry.

Some people stood for a time before the tableau; others knelt, leaning against the railing. With some the moment was brief, a mere pause and then the return; with others it was longer. Some walked away in precisely the manner with which they had approached; with others the pace was altogether different. He wished he could see more of their faces, but from his position in the church and from the angle of their turning, he could catch only a moving glimpse and that was always after the moment of truth, if that was what it was.

The problem he set himself was to try to determine the nature of the person and the particular challenge being faced by the movement toward the manger, the position when before it, and the way the return to the body of the church was made. He reached into his pocket for notebook and pencil, then remembered he had given up carrying them when he had gone to work in the factory. All he had was a pocket diary and there was little space in it, as it was so near the end of the year. He would have to impress what he was observing so on his mind that he could write it down when he got back to his room.

Now there was no one at the manger and a glance up the aisle told him no one was on the way. He slipped out of his seat and walked as casually toward the front of the church as if he had done it countless times before. Standing before the tableau with his arms across his chest and his feet apart, he studied the scene; not because there was anything new about it but because it was like every manger scene in Christendom, like

Christmas cards, like the pictures in Christmas books. Odd, that no one ever changed it, modernized it, did something to it to make it different; then he corrected himself. It couldn't be any different, it had to be like this; it had to speak to people as it was, as it might have been on that first night in Bethlehem.

"Did you know," he asked the sleeping Babe, "what you were born to do? Bet not; bet you were just a happy kid growing up with others in your village until—" His mind went back over the story. "How old were you, twelve was it, when they found you in the temple and you told them you had to be about your Father's business? You knew then, and you went ahead, and your whole heart was in your work. You knew they'd catch up with you before long but you didn't care, for what mattered to you was to get on with the thing you were born to do."

He paused, almost as if he expected the baby to open his eyes and look at him with the wise expression those too young to speak often have; but it didn't. In fact, he was no longer aware of the scene before him, for the scene in the factory manager's office a few hours earlier had become vivid. He had been asked to stop in before leaving, and he knew what was meant by the request.

The manager had been polite, more than polite, kindly; he had given him the check that was lying on the desk, he had shaken hands and wished him well. Almost as an afterthought he had said, "We're sorry to have to let you go, but your heart isn't in this kind of work." As he stood before the manger and relived the factory scene, he wondered if he would hear the echo of those words in another few months, and then in another. His heart never would be in precision work, or in selling, or in figures, or in any of the things many men did to make a living. What twisted reasoning was it that kept him trying everything except the one thing he really wanted to do? He shook his head as if to feint off the answer.

Turning, he walked back up the aisle, glad he had left his coat bunched up on the seat or he might not have been able to find where he had been sitting.

To anyone watching her, she would not have seemed to walk so much as float, waft, drift down the aisle to the manger. She was tall and thin, her fair hair hung to her shoulders and rested on her black coat. At the manger, she knelt and bowed her head for the space of time needed for her prayer. This was the first day she had been out since the news had come three weeks ago about Jerry. She had not been able to see the Government representative when he had called. Her parents had listened to the story and tried to tell it to her later, tried to explain to her about Jerry's insurance, and all the other details; but she could not listen. She had cried all night that first night, and spasmodically, uncontrollably, during the next few days. When she reached a point where there were no more tears, she was conscious of the ache within her as if the tears had somehow eased it. Her parents mentioned going to the Candle-light Service and she had said she would like to go with them. They had looked at her uncertainly, tenderly, and she had assured them that she would be all right. Tears were behind her now, and with them all feeling.

She wondered if she would ever cry again. Nothing that life could do to her in all the years she might have to live would ever be like this : to lose Jerry was to lose her hold on life. Older people, her parents for instance, might die and leave her temporarily bereft; but that would be normal, in the fullness of time with their lives well lived. Jerry's life had been cut off almost before he had had a chance to live, and with his hers, too.

But she would not have missed the Candlelight Service, it had been a part of her for so long. She had come first in her mother's arms, so she had been told; then she had toddled up to the manger with other children; later she had walked more demurely. Last year she and Jerry had gone up together and knelt before the familiar scene. Looking at the baby, she had wondered if Jerry was thinking as she was, that someday—in a year or two or three—they, too, would have a little one; but their baby would not sleep on hay in a wooden manger but in a bassinet with white sheets and the softest of blankets. Pink? Blue? The tears she had thought would never form again began to blur her vision.

The church had been a background to her life for as long as she could remember. Her first public appearance had been as a flower girl at the wedding of one of her aunts. So absorbed had she been by the pattern of the carpet and the need to step in time with the music that she had com-

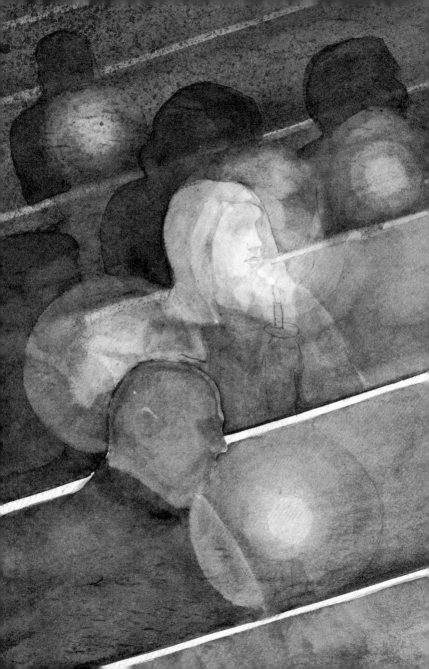

pletely forgotten to scatter any rose petals as she walked. Reaching the step before the altar and realizing that her basket was still full, she had tipped it in one place and made a carpet of petals for the bride to stand on. There had been the many festivals of the year and through the year; there had been the many different occasions culminating in her's and Jerry's wedding last June, three days after graduation from high school and three weeks before he left for training camp.

She stared at the baby through misted eyes. Never would she carry one under her heart; only her sorrow would she carry there always. "When I come back," Jerry had said, "when we can have our own home, when—when—when—" But he had not come back, not even for a funeral, though there had been a memorial service a few days after the news had been received. The Government representative had been sympathetic, almost as if he were personally responsible, when he explained to her parents what had happened; but the grim fact remained that after the explosion there had been no survivors.

Alone, kneeling before the manger, life looked bleak as it stretched before her, loveless without

Jerry; for there would never be anyone to take his place.

The scene that had taken her back to her childhood and arrested time arrested grief momentarily. Before the marvel of the newborn, everything within her became still in adoration. On this night, and only for these few hours, no one thought of what lay ahead—the secret journey into Egypt, the cruel journey up to Calvary. From shepherds to kings, including all that lay between, joy was felt that the child long promised had come at last. The sleeping figure in the manger was wrapped in the love of those who were near him, even the gentle beasts, as surely as he was in the woven cloth that covered him. Some excess of that love seemed to overflow the stable, seemed to wrap her in its warmth.

She wished that she had something to give to the Babe. A line from a poem learned years ago crossed her mind—"Little smiles and little tears are all we've brought." She had nothing to give him but her empty, aching heart, so she gave it.

The sound of someone coming down the aisle reminded her that she must yield her place at the manger. It was a careful sound, as of one very sure of his direction. She rose from her kneeling position, turned around and caught tentative smiles from the faces of Jerry's young brother and sister who were sitting in the front pew. She smiled back at them, then glided up the aisle to take her place beside her parents.

He came down the aisle slowly, as if each step were seen inwardly before the next one was taken. His left hand, held sideways, touched each pew as he passed but so unobtrusively that unless an onlooker knew this was his way of approach it would seem that in walking so to the left of the aisle he merely brushed the pews as he passed them; his right arm, its elbow bent, was held slightly out from his body, ready to cushion or to greet. At the first pew he paused and tilted his head. A scent, a flow of warmth from the candle at one side of the manger scene, gave him direction and he moved forward into the area between the front of the pew and the railing. He tilted his head again for the feel of the candle at the far side, then he spaced himself between the candles and stood in front of the manger, breathing the freshness of the flowers. Feeling with the tips of his shoes, he gauged the height of the kneeling bench and dropped to it gracefully.

The eyes of many people in the church had been following him, watching how precisely and without pause in the flow of his movement he had placed himself exactly where he wanted to be; others, so used to seeing him do this year after year, thought nothing of the procedure and became more intent on finding places in their hymnals, as the service was soon to start.

He did not bow his head as many others had. He kept his head up as if he would observe the whole, since each part contributed to it. He had never seen it, except in the eye of his mind where he saw it very well. Mary's robe was silver-gray, like the sky, like the sea, like distant mountains; Joseph's was golden-brown, like the earth or the trunks of trees. The baby's hair was a pure white halo, and the cloth that covered him was every-color. The hay, the sweet fragrant hay that lined the manger and lay over the floor, was a field of blue flowers. It did not matter what people told him about the scene; he knew it as he saw it inwardly.

He knew the figures better than anyone, since for many years it had been his special task, when the scene was dismantled, to clean them, wrap them in cloth, and put them away to be ready for another year. They were old, older than the church's oldest member but not so old as the church, and fragile. His fingers were sensitive and could be trusted to handle even the most delicate objects with care. A newcomer to the town, when told of how the figures were cared for and who did it, had said, "Well now, isn't that nice, it gives that poor old man something to do." But nobody in the town thought that way. They were glad there was someone with love in his fingers who could be relied on not only to clean and oil the wood but to make any needed repairs.

His shoulders erect and his head uplifted, he did not look like an old man as he knelt by the manger, nor did he look suppliant; rather he looked like someone ready and waiting for his name to be called.

He did not remain long. The organ voluntary had come to a close and the organist was playing the music of the first carol that would be sung. He rose to stand and then turned, right arm slightly forward to feel for the front of the first pew; then, with direction assured, he retraced his steps into

the aisle. Lightly touching each pew end and counting them—seven—eleven—fourteen, he turned again and settled into the seat he had left a few minutes ago. A hand reached out to brush against his to tell him that he was in his right place. Those who were near enough to see his face found themselves smiling with him. He looked as if he had seen something that could not be kept entirely to himself.

Now, with the singing of the first of several carols, the Candlelight Service commenced. As the manger scene was the same year after year, so was the pattern of the service. Prophecies from the Old Testament were read and their fulfillment in the New. It was a well-known story. Most of the people in the church had heard it many times, but they listened to it like children; like children, they became involved in it. Through the reading from the pulpit, through the singing from the congregation, through the motionless figures of the tableau, came the feeling that on this night and because of it everyone had a chance to begin again: to be born into life as the Babe had been born, to grow into manhood as he had grown in self-giving.

During the meditation the organ played softly, so the music would not intrude but only lightly guide, the Pastoral from the *Messiah* and then the air "He shall feed his flock . . . and gently lead those that are with young." Some knew or could recall the words, and, thinking them with the music, offered them as prayer. The organ rippled into the Bach chorale "Jesu, Joy of Man's Desiring," and all who were present—no matter what sorrow or shame, pressure or loss or fear weighed upon them—felt like Mary and heart-pondered the things that had been heard.

Then the great moment came when the candles were given out, each one cupped in a cardboard collar. The ushers handed them to all but a very few. By long-established custom, candles were never given to children under ten; so, among those who were present, the little girl who stood between her parents put her hand on her mother's and pretended that she was holding her own. The blind man did not hold a candle for that same custom had decreed that one might not be safe in his hands; and the bearded man in the back row had refused one, whispering to the usher that he had to leave before the service was over. Candle holders at the aisle side of each pew received their lights from tapers held by the ushers; then from wick to wick in each pew the candles were lit, and soon the body of the church was pricked with a hundred points of light. Faces glowed like a garden of golden flowers.

"Now, let us say our Litany of Light," came the voice from the pulpit. As each verse was read, it was then repeated by the congregation—

"The spirit of man is the candle of the Lord."

"For thou wilt light my candle: the Lord my God will enlighten my darkness."

"Arise, shine; for thy light is come."

"Jesus said unto them, Yet a little while is the light with you. Walk while ye have the light . . ."

"Believe in the light that ye may be the children of light."

"If we walk in the light, as he is in the light, we have fellowship one with another . . ."

"Lord, lift thou up the light of thy countenance upon us."

Some, listening to the familiar words, repeated them as part of a ritual; others, taking them to their hearts as a personal message, said them as if they were marriage vows.

Then the charge was given: "So walk, each one of you in the light of your candle, reverently with respect for all things holy, expectantly for this is a time of great blessing."

The organ did not peal out in a postlude of joyous abandon; such strains would be for the morrow. This was the night when a Babe was sleeping in a manger; the hour when many carried in their hearts hope of new birth. From its medley of carols, the organ moved in an almost sprightly manner into the music of "Lead, Kindly Light." Those who knew the words sang them as they left their pews; others hummed the tune. Some were ready to leave for their homes; others who had not yet visited the manger moved forward in the church, holding their candles carefully. Those who carried their candles toward the door and into the night endeavored to keep them alight as long as possible.

". . . Keep thou my feet, I do not ask to see
The distant scene—one step enough for me."

That was how it would have to be : as one step
was taken the next would be revealed, and then
the next . . . and then the next. Darkness
would yield to the light and the way would
become clear.

TWO

IN THE STREET

The bearded man in the last row was the first to leave. He pushed open the door and stood on the step to get his direction, holding his head high as if some element of self-respect had been temporarily restored to him. As his eyes followed the row of streetlights up to the intersection and then came back to the area near the church, he was aware of a man standing near the bottom step.

"You're late, stranger," he said. "Service is just over. People will all be coming out soon."

The stranger said something about beginning again and seemed disposed to talk, but the bearded man had no desire to linger.

"Church won't be having another service," he muttered as he moved down the steps; "not enough people in this town to warrant that." Brushing by the stranger, he went along the walk in his catfooted way. He had thought to get back to the main street by an unlighted side street, but instead, following an impulse, he decided to walk up to the intersection and then down the lighted main street. After all, he had nothing to conceal tonight. He'd kept his hands away from the woman's purse in the church, even though he could well have used a few of the dollars it must have contained.

His hands were cold, so he thrust them into his pockets for warmth. The sensation of what the left one closed around jolted him to action. Better get rid of it, he told himself, then he would feel like a decent man. He looked around him to make certain that no one was near. Everyone in the town must have been at the service, for the street ahead of him was as empty as it might be at midnight. Behind him he could see people coming from the church, standing on the steps and talking together, holding their candles, making a little cluster of radiance in the night. He tried to find the stranger among them but couldn't distinguish him in the crowd.

With a deft motion, he took his left hand from his pocket and tossed the angular object into a snowbank. He didn't look to see where it had landed but walked on down the main street. It might have weighed ten pounds rather than as many ounces for the relief he felt when he got rid of it. He should have known better, he chided himself, than to filch a child's toy; but there it had been, standing by the door, waiting to be picked up. It had struck him that he might give it to his mother as a present. A toy might suit her fancy. Now he had nothing to give her.

So far ahead was he of the people coming from the church and so deserted was the street that he began to walk in a more leisurely fashion, putting one foot down fully, then the other. He was surprised and rather pleased to feel the support the ground gave him. He went on past the post office, past the public library given by his grandfather. The name he bore, when he wasn't using an alias, was the same as the name carved on the stone front of the building. He stared at it, confronted by the fact. Turning left, he went down the short street to the bridge that crossed the river. There he stopped to lean against the rail and look ahead of him to the nursing home. It stood on a rise of land, its windows lighted, a tree on its lawn hung with colored lights.

The river was covered with a film of ice. It was the river he had skated on as a boy, and swum in

and fished. There was an old boat he and his friends used to row upstream to a place where the river had carved out a cove. The water was deep there, always still and shadowed by huge willows. That was where they caught the best fish. His right hand, fingering the small revolver, brought it out and he stared at it. Confronted again by a fact, he found it hard to believe that he had once thought it spelled safety. It didn't look to him now as it once had. He felt ashamed of it, as if it were something unclean. He glanced around, half-thinking that the stranger might have followed him, half-wishing that he had so they could talk together. But there was no one.

Had the stranger said that *he* could begin again? In his desire to move on, he might have misunderstood him in the darkness.

With a gesture as vigorous as any he had used when a boy on the baseball team, he pitched the revolver from him into the river. It landed with a flat thud on the ice. He watched it as it lay there, barely visible. He watched it as a cold horror crept through him. What if it was not obliterated by the water? What if it was discovered tomorrow? Fingerprints would be taken. It would be known to whom it belonged, and then that he had been in town. There was a faint shivering sound, a slight sagging as the ice began to give way. Slowly the bearded man let out the breath he had been holding; slowly the revolver sank out of sight. Fascinated, he watched the small whirlpool created by the breaking ice before the water stilled. Only a black hole remained and the ice would close it in again by morning.

His hands were free now and with them he smoothed his hair, felt for his tie to straighten it. Swinging away from the river, he faced the lighted house on the hill and started toward it; he walked proudly as his grandfather might have walked in the town's early days. He had nothing for his mother but his hands were clean. He remembered how often she had told him when he was a boy to wash his hands before a meal; doing so, he would hold them out to show them to her. Perhaps, when he saw her tonight, he would hold out his hands in the old way. By that gesture she might know him and not be put off by the beard. She might even laugh at it as if it were a child's masquerade.

He walked briskly, but the hill was steep enough to slow his pace. He kept his head high and his eyes on the lighted windows of the house he was approaching. Something lost long ago had been found.

The child walked in step with her parents, each one holding a lighted candle, to the door of the church. The double radiance made a pool of light that encircled her and cast its glow well ahead. Once outside, there was enough light to see down the steps but little beyond. On the edge of the darkness a man was standing, and the little girl knew that if she missed a step he would catch her. She had been quiet long enough. Now she wanted to run.

"I'll get home before you!" she sang out as she darted away from her parents and down the steps.

She would have fallen at the last one if a strong arm had not reached out to hold and steady her, then send her on her way. "Keep your eyes wide open," a kindly voice said.

"I will!" she responded gaily as she flung herself into the night.

She ran with joy and confidence over a familiar way until a twinge of conscience slowed her down, then stopped her altogether. She had not thanked the man who had kept her from falling, and she was old enough to know that kindness should always be acknowledged. Spinning around, she flung a "thank you" into the night; but when she saw how many people there were on the church steps, she wondered if he would ever hear it.

"Oh well, he'll know I meant to say thank you," she persuaded herself, "and I shall keep my eyes wide open."

From that point she walked more deliberately, knowing that she would still get home long before her mother and father. She had nothing to slow her down and they would walk carefully as they tried to keep their candles alight for as long as possible. With so much time, she decided to go the long way home. That meant going all the way up to the intersection, crossing there, then taking the street that led past her school and circled around to come out by her house. She ran again, creating a small breeze in the stillness of the night; but at the intersection she came to a halt and looked four ways for traffic. There was none except for the cars that were coming away from the church.

She waited for one that came crawling like a

tortoise up to the intersection. She could see the passenger in the front seat holding two candles while the driver was being very considerate. The car began flicking to indicate a left turn, but it was approaching so slowly that the little girl felt she would be waiting forever for it, so she made two crossings instead of the one she had intended : the first ahead to the right, then the second to the left. Even at that, the car had not yet made its turn. She waited again to watch it go by and waved to its occupants.

As it turned, the headlights rested on a snow-bank, lighting up not so much the snow as an object lying on the snow. After the car had passed, the little girl went to investigate. Then she stood very still.

"My horse!" she gasped. "My little wooden horse!" She approached it and knelt against the snowbank to retrieve it.

Taking it in her hands, she brushed off the snow from its mane and tail; she ran her fingers over the body and down the legs; then she held it close to her. She couldn't understand what was happening to her. When she had knelt at the manger to pray, and had told the sleeping Babe how she had lost her horse, she had cried. Now

she was crying because she had found her horse.

Three people, walking slowly with their candles, called her by name. "Your parents will be along soon. They stopped to talk to someone as they came out of church."

She nodded. Whatever she had thought about getting home first had gone from her. Now all she could think of was to get back to her parents. She watched the people go down the street, walking in the light of their candles. After they had gone, she looked again at what she held tightly in her hands and close to her body. It was true. He was hers again. She crooned to him in their secret language and rubbed her nose against his handsome head.

Turning about face, she crossed the intersection the direct way and went back toward the church, threading herself in and out among the clusters of people. Many candles still burned, a few had already done their work and gone out. Finding her parents, she stood before them and held up her toy for them to see.

"Look!" she demanded.

"You did run fast to get home and back here again so soon!"

"Did you find him where you thought you had put him?"

She shook her head and pointed toward the intersection. "There—on top of a snowbank—there—" It was all she could say.

They turned to face each other uncomprehendingly, then they looked at their daughter. The candles they held were more than half gone but there was light enough to see the wonder in her eyes and the tear-stained joy of her face.

"I prayed to find him," she said simply, then more slowly as this was hard to say; "I told the baby when I did I would bring him my horse to play with."

There was such stillness around the three that, for a moment, they might have been the only people in the world.

Hand on the little girl's shoulder, her mother said, "The Babe is asleep now. Tomorrow will be the time for gift giving."

"Yes, tomorrow," her father repeated. "We will come early and you may place your horse in the manger."

Slowly a smile spread across the child's face. Her fingers tightened. For a little while longer she would have her wooden horse. Nodding, she took her place between her parents for the walk home.

They looked at each other over the small head.

"How——ever——" Lips shaped the words.

Almost more with his eyes than with his lips, the little girl's father said, "Let's not question a miracle, but," with his free hand he made an inward turning gesture, "accept it."

Her heels clicking sharply behind her, she moved through the open door and started rapidly down the steps. The candle she held went out. With an exclamation of annoyance she started to toss it away. An acquaintance, coming through the door and seeing her plight, leaned toward her with a light.

"Thanks," she murmured, wondering why she had involved herself again with such a troublesome thing as a candle. Standing still to let the flame strengthen, she watched people as they went down the steps then did what she saw them do, shielded the candle with her free hand and kept her eyes on its wavering flame. When she started down the steps, her attention became riveted on the way the candle did what the words of the hymn had said. It revealed one step and showed how the next could be taken.

Reaching the bottom step, she walked ahead briskly. The flame trembled, lowered itself into the pool of wax at its base, and almost fluttered out.

"Take your time," a man's voice could be heard, then a hand was held gently toward the flame until it grew strong again.

"How can I!" she exclaimed. "I've taken so much time already. I'm late as it is."

"For what?"

Her candle began to burn steadily again. It gave enough light for her to see where she was going, but nothing beyond the next step or two and nothing on her right or left. In spite of the many people who had been coming from the church, there seemed to be no one anywhere near her except the man who had protected her light; and him she could not see. His voice was vaguely familiar, but she couldn't remember ever having met anyone recently with a voice like his. She supposed he was a visitor in town, or a newcomer who had attended the Candlelight Service for the first time. He might be in need of some information, so she asked if she could do anything for him.

No, he said, thanking her and adding that he

wanted to walk beside her for a while to keep her candle from going out, and to talk.

"I haven't time to talk. I've so much to do. I never should have come out tonight."

"Do?"

"Oh, you should see my room with all the presents I have to wrap up!"

"What would happen if you didn't wrap them?"

"Didn't—" she gasped, then realized that even emphatic words could take a toll from her candle flame. In the pause exacted, she thought of the packages in her room. After all, it was the contents that mattered. The gay wrapping and big bows added only a personal touch to the present itself. Perhaps it wasn't as important as she had thought, especially when time was short.

"Yes," she said thoughtfully, "I see what you mean. But, even if I give up the wrappings, there are so many cards I ought to write. I won't get to bed before midnight, if then."

"Cards?" The note of questioning hung on the air. "Ways of remembrance. But why only tonight?"

"Why! Because it's—" Again the candle warned her of its tenuous life. The question took hold of her and she asked herself why the act of remembering should be confined to a certain season. It might be more meaningful to spread it through the year with letters written at less crowded times, letters that would carry more of herself than a few words and a name on a card.

"Yes." Almost against her will but in keeping with her judgment, she found herself being persuaded. "Well," she said, "say I forget about wrappings and cards this year, there's the tree to trim and that always takes an hour or more."

"A tree is beautiful in itself, as it comes from the forest, straight, green, fragrant."

"I really haven't time to think about things like this, tonight of all nights." Her words were spoken firmly but with respect for the candle flame.

"Time? What is it but a growing into eternity."

The voice sounded from behind her so she waited for him to come up alongside her again, and as she waited she began to see time in a different light, time as a space for growing. Her insistence had begun to yield and she was ready to admit that there probably always would be time enough for the things that mattered.

"Who are you?" she whispered, turning

around and holding her candle at arm's length to see his face. There was no one there. Beyond the circle of light, the night was dark, impenetrable, kind.

Drawing her hand back she looked at the candle, trying to estimate its length of burning. Now, all that mattered to her was to keep it alight until it lived its length, until it had served the purpose for which it was intended. If she continued to walk as she had since she came down the steps, it would see her home.

At the next corner, she took a shortcut through an empty lot. It was a way she rarely took, as the going was rough and she was not able to walk as rapidly as she could along the street; but she was obliged to walk slowly in any case if she would keep her candle alive. Even though the newcomer had left her and she no longer had his questions to prod her mind, she discovered there was a great deal she wanted to think about: things made clear by the light of the candle yet things she had always known. In her thinking she kept returning to an awareness of that secret place beyond the things of time wherein one lived to be made ready for eternity.

Halfway across the lot she saw pinpricks of

light in the distance, moving as if to approach her. As they came nearer, she saw that it was a procession of three candles, the holders of them walking as reverently as she was. It was not until they were all quite close that she saw who they were—Roger and the two children.

When they met and their several lights merged into one, Roger said, "We weren't sure that you would come this way, but we hoped you would."

"Mummy, we brought another candle for you!"

It was held up to take light from the one she carried that was near the end of its burning. In the new light she looked at them. The children's eyes were shining. Like stars, she thought, as she gazed at one then the other. She leaned over to kiss them, then straightening up she slipped her arm through Roger's as all four turned toward home.

She stood on the steps near her parents, conscious of the soft-voiced greetings, the gentle way people spoke to her as if a little embarrassed by her presence. She had no words at her command, only a "Thanks" shaped by her lips and a re-focusing of her eyes. It was not easy to face people, however kindly intentioned they were. She wondered if it would ever be. It was not easy to carry out her intent, but she felt that she must at least try.

Looking at her parents she said, "I'm not going home with you."

They seemed surprised.

"I'm going around to see Jerry's folks. His brother and sister were at the service. It's been a long time—" her voice trailed off uncertainly.

They smiled at her, trying not to appear too pleased at what they had heard. She had not wanted to see her parents-in-law and her decision now cheered them, making them feel that perhaps the tide of shock and grief was turning to acceptance.

"God bless," they murmured as they remained on the top step and watched her move into the darkness.

She held her candle before her face and quite high; some of its light fell on her fair hair, giving an effect of more light. She walked effortlessly with the curious lilt to her step that gave the appearance of her being wafted more by a roving wind than her own power of movement. Others standing on the steps stood back and watched her go, following her with their eyes and their hearts.

"Poor dear," more than one murmured and as many thought, "to have to face such a loss."

Older people were used to sorrow and learned to bear it with a kind of nobility; with the young it was awkwardly borne, like a garment that did not fit.

Halfway down the short walk that led out to the street, she hesitated. Leaving the manger her intention had been strong to go and see Jerry's mother; now she found it weakening. Uncertain of herself, unsure of her direction, she sighed. Her candle was held so close to her face that the slight escape of breath blew it out.

Almost before she could adjust herself to the lack of light, she realized that the pleasant voice of someone on her left was offering to light her candle. Surprised, for she thought she had come down the steps and into the night alone, she mumbled thanks as she saw the light approach her black wick and the cupped hand that shielded it. Gradually the flame became strong and light shedding. Her eyes looked one way, but her feet started in another. She stopped as if to decide what was her way.

"You've lost something?"

The voice came from beyond the rim of light so she could not see who was speaking to her. She felt as if she had heard it before. It sounded almost like Jerry's, not so much in its tone as in its tenderness.

She moved her head slowly, up and down. "I—" She caught her breath, wondering if she should say what lay so deep in her heart. "I don't have anything to live for."

"Live?" The word rested on the air like a long-drawn note of music. "We live because we are one with life, one with love."

"Oh," she shuddered, "please don't speak to me about love. I can't bear it."

"You were going somewhere. You mustn't stand here long or your light will be spent."

"My heart tells me to do one thing, but everything else tells me to do another. Even my feet would have me go home the quickest, shortest way, the way I came to the service."

"Follow your heart."

Her answer was given as she started forward in the direction her eyes had been looking.

His footsteps companioned her and helped to give her confidence.

"Are you going this way, too?"

"Yes, I'm going your way."

"Oh, I am glad. I get so lonely. Sometimes I think I can't stand life with no one to love."

"And you think that love can be confined to one human being?"

"Yes," she said, "Jerry." It was easy to be honest in the dark and her words flowed from her readily. The near presence of the one whose face she could not see was curiously comforting and she had the feeling that he cared. "Jerry and I had known each other since we were children. When we were married—it's hard to explain, but—it was as if there had never been a time when we hadn't been one. I needed him so much, and he needed me, and life was bliss. Now—" she drew her breath in quickly "—life without him looks very long, and bleak, and dark."

"Where the candle glows?"

"No. Light is there, but it is so small."

"But it is enough."

"For one step, of course." She could agree with him about something so obvious.

"How many more do you ever have to take at one time?"

"I—I—" She wanted to parry the question in

some way but found that she could not. "No more," she answered, subdued by her own reason.

They walked on in silence except for the sound of their footsteps.

"You don't understand," she began again. "Jerry needed someone to believe in him the way I did."

"Each one who walks the earth needs that."

"And I—I needed his love."

"Each one who walks the earth needs that."

"He gave me so much."

"What are you going to do with all that he gave?"

"Please," she said, "I can't answer that yet."

The compassionate voice continued and she listened humbly. If life had any lesson to teach it was that we are here to learn love and to be givers of love. If death had any lesson to teach it was that love was only rarefied, intensified.

"Tonight, at the manger, I had nothing to give but an empty heart," she said.

"And you gave it that it might be filled."

"Yes." She recalled how clearly the intent had come to her to go where she was now going. "Only as I follow the little lead will the way open for the next to appear," she told herself, comforted by her own knowledge.

Her eyes had not left the candle flame since the wick had been relit for her. It had burned down almost to its paper collar, but it would last as long as she required it. For some time she had realized that she was walking alone, but she did not feel lonely. One thought out of all the many that had been in her mind became increasingly clear : Love was always being born again, like the Babe this holy night, and love yearned to be received. What she had lost she would pine for no longer; instead she would live what had been richly given her and so doing affirm life. She had always known this must be so, even in the midst of her sorrow; but something had happened to her on this starlit, candlelit night to unlock her heart and set her free.

As she approached the house, she came within the glow of its light and had no further need of her candle. Going up to the door she put her hand on the bell, then hesitated. Announce her arrival and in another moment she would be surrounded by people who loved her and who did not withhold their love—Jerry's folks. There might even be others there, too, for the house was always

full. She turned to glance down the street to see if her companion might be lingering anywhere.

A man with his head bent slightly toward his flickering candle was walking up the path to the house. She had seen him with his heavy thatch of hair and squared shoulders when he went to the manger and idly wondered who he might be. This was not the man who had walked beside her in the darkness. Dropping her hand to her side, she waited.

Snuffing his candle temporarily to conserve it, he leaned against the doorpost to watch the people as they emerged from the church. Evidently it was difficult for some to walk slowly enough to keep their candles burning; others walked as if their lives depended on it. Reflecting on the people he observed, he realized that many a lesson was being learned in the course of that downward flight of steps. Most of the congregation, he decided, must have things to do, reasons to get home, friends and families to enjoy on this particular night. He had nothing to do so he could afford to take his time, nothing until he went out to look for another job the day after Christmas;

yet he had everything to do that he personally liked.

Unnoticed in the shadow, he surveyed the people, trying to decide what their lives were, their aims, their needs, their predicaments. Again he wished that he had a notebook with him and reminded himself that he must start carrying one; again he tried to make impressions go deep so that when he got back to his room he could write them down, though what he would do with them he did not know. Nothing probably; they would go the way of everything he had written during the last few years.

All around him there was a pervasive air of well-wishing: smiles, handclasps, greetings. People weren't their real selves tonight; then he caught himself. Perhaps they were more their real selves. Mellowed by the music, the candlelight, the words sung and heard, the memories stirred at the manger, they had become utterly natural, as the pressures under which they lived much of the time slid away.

The stream emerging from the church had gone down to a trickle, composed mostly of older folk who did not entice his imagination as much as did people in their early or middle years.

With most of them, problems had been solved and in their faces their stories were written clearly.

"May I?" he held his candle toward a woman just coming out the door.

"Certainly," she smiled as she brought her flame toward his wick and waited until she was sure the light had caught.

His eyes followed her down the steps and into the night, then shielding his candle he went on his way. He had come to the church along the road that followed the river, but he decided to return to the house where he had a room by the shortest way. Only so could he be sure that the candle would last. Sensible of a man keeping pace with him, he felt that it was just another of the pleasant things that happened on Christmas Eve when people seemed to live outside their own concerns for a while.

"Familiar with the town?" he asked by way of acknowledging a presence that was beyond his line of vision.

"Yes, indeed."

"Can't say I am too much. I've been here only a few weeks. Came to take a job in the electronics factory."

"Do you like it?"

"Not the job. The town's all right, but I won't be here much longer."

"Why?"

For a moment he took his eyes from his candle to see his questioner, but beyond the outline of a tall figure the darkness was all enveloping.

"I lost my job today."

"Oh, you did!" There was no regret in the voice, no sympathy. Its inflection was congratulatory. "Why?"

Piqued by what seemed like callous curiosity, the young man squared his shoulders even more than was habitual; but instead of brushing off the question with an evasive answer, he found that in justice to himself he wanted to make some kind of reply.

"Why? Because I wasn't any good at it. My heart just isn't in assembling components, but there's money in it and I need that."

"Why?"

"Because I want to get married and that takes money."

"What is your heart in?"

"People. I like to observe them, watch what they do and try to figure out their reasons. I like to imagine them in different situations and then try to determine what would happen if—if—you know all the 'ifs' you can toss into a situation."

"You want to write."

"You've got my idea, friend, and I'm going to someday."

"Why not now?"

"I just told you. I've got to have a paying job so I can get married."

"Oh—" The sound carried neither question nor exclamation. The voice had become increasingly familiar, but try as he would the young man could not seem to attach a name to it.

"The girl I'm engaged to likes to live well."

"Each one must do what he came into the world equipped to do."

"Is everyone equipped in some way?"

"God is not a partial giver."

"Does everyone recognize his gift?"

"Some do easily; with others it takes courage. When courage is lacking, life becomes a treadmill rather than a journey."

"If I don't ask her to marry me soon, she'll settle for someone else."

"If she believed in you . . . ?"

The question hung on the air. The only answer was a defensive one. "A man has to make a living."

To that there was no reply.

"Maybe what you're trying to say to me is that I've got to believe in myself before I can expect anyone else to believe in me, that some-time or other I've got to do what I really want to do."

A casual conversation had become a heated discussion. The more the young man talked, the more he began to believe in himself.

"There's no use sliding along on old excuses. I'll have to take the risk, prove that I've got courage. Money isn't everything. I can't go on any longer saying I'll make some and then write. I'll have to forget about money, and write."

He felt like laughing at himself. Only a little while ago he had been wondering what he would do with Christmas Day other than study want ads in all the papers he could put his hands on. He knew now that he would write. There would be hours and hours of free time; beyond making a few long-distance calls and having dinner with the family where he was living, the day would be all his.

Before he turned off the main street, he thrust his candle sideways with a sudden movement. "Thanks, friend. I thought I'd lost my job. Now I guess I've found the only one I've ever really wanted to do."

There was no one there and he was oddly unsurprised. The casual walker had said nothing unusual anyway, only made him aware of what he had always known.

As he approached the house, he saw a girl standing on the doorstep, the light from a near lamp shedding its glow around her. He had noticed her at the service. She was one of the ones who had intrigued his mind.

"Are you coming here, too?" she asked.

"Yes, I've got a room here."

The wick of his candle was flaring in the pool of wax at its base, then with a faintly audible sound it went out; but there was no longer any need for light.

"Strange," he said, as he rolled the softened wax into its paper collar, "I thought that I was walking with someone for a while."

"So did I."

He could not resist, as she had not been able to a few moments earlier, the desire to gaze back the way he had come, peering into the night. From a recess he had had no occasion to turn to for a long time, he withdrew some remembered lines—

"And looking back—at that short space—
Could see a glimpse of His bright face."

"Oh," she caught her breath, "do you like poetry?"

"Yes, I do." Then without shyness or embarrassment, and as simply as he might have said that he drove a car, he announced, "I write poetry."

The look she turned on him was luminous.

"Were you waiting for me?" he asked.

"No, but when I saw you coming I decided to wait. On a winter's night it lets less cold into a house if the door has to open only once instead of twice."

He was used to waiting, used to being last. It was often better that way; easier for others and easier for him. So he sat peacefully in the pew halfway back in the church as the people began to leave, some for the door and some for the journey that had not yet been made to Bethlehem. Sounds that had filled the building began to fall away: the shuffling of many feet dwindled to that of a few, and then only those few on the steps outside as they went into the night. The organ had become softer until it seemed to be only a whisper of sound, and then an echo, and then the sound was not outside him but within.

Awareness came in exquisite ways. There had been warmth from the many small candles and fragrance; but there was no near warmth now, and the scent had changed as it lingered on the air. Only the two tall candles at the manger and those on the altar were still alight. He tilted his face to catch their fragrance. It was different, richer than that from the small candles. He could hear footsteps from the direction of the vestry. Someone was coming to extinguish the candles and close the church.

He stood up in the pew so it would not seem as if he had fallen asleep. Unwilling to go, yet knowing he must, he turned and went up the aisle, brushing the pew ends with his arm and counting. When he got to the open space, he moved easily forward the half-dozen steps necessary to reach the door. Once there, it gave to his touch and he stood outside, breathing in the sharp air that was so different from the close, warm air of the church. He could hear a few fading footsteps in the distance and the murmur of voices, then both ceased. The winter night that held the town in its grip had distilled sound into silence. He extended his left arm a little way from his body, hand partly open as if it were holding a candle in its paper collar.

"Thy word is a lamp unto my feet, and a light unto my path." It was the prayer he said at night and in the morning, for the darkness and the light were both alike.

Centering himself by the feel of the door at his back, he started forward, his steps measured, his tread certain. In the church behind him the lights began to go out. A wind that had not been up a few moments earlier blew through the street. He slanted his face to it, glad of it. It came off the river, and even though the river was running under ice, it still lent dampness to the air. If he kept the wind at his back, it would help to get him over the first part of his journey, and it was not far : two turns to make and a short hill to ascend.

Cognizant of the presence beside him, he felt no need for conversation. Life had long been warmed by close companionship, and though words were richly enjoyed there was always a time when they became superfluous, when they intruded on some rare wholeness. He lived in the memory of that companionship and in the certitude of its renewal.

Before making the first turn at the corner, he paused. A mailbox was there and he ran his hand over it in a gesture of friendship. Now the wind was off his right shoulder, which was as it should be. By the time he turned again, the wind would be full in his face.

The coin of life had been his for a long time and he knew one side of it well. Soon it would be time for turning and he would be able to see what the other side held. He had learned to check his impatience, for the turning could not be hastened. There was only one way to advance, the way of the last hymn they had sung at the Candlelight Service, a step, and another, and another. That was the way he was walking now, though he carried no candle to part the darkness. It would take more than a candle to do that for him.

"—one step enough for me." He hummed the tune as he went along.

Such a simple thing it was to do, quite as simple as bending the knees in obeisance to that little figure in the manger; obedience came harder. It

took all of life to learn that. Again he paused, again he reached for that which marked his turn, this time the post of a streetlight. Now the wind was in his face and his feet felt the upwardness of the path.

Before he resumed his way, he turned half-circle to look at the one who walked beside him. In the depths of eyes whose gaze held his, he saw what he had dreamed of seeing : not what he was as in a mirror, but face to face what he would be.

Around him light streamed. The cold dissolved, and the snow, and even the town that huddled into itself for warmth. There was nothing but light and a field of blue flowers that waved in a singing breeze. He started to run through the ankle-high flowers, knowing that his feet would leave no trace nor crush their bloom; after he had gone by, they would wave as gallantly in the breeze as they had when he first saw them.

Among the many legends that have to do with Christmas Eve, there is one that says on that night lost things are found again.

References

Page 40   From "How Far Is It to Bethlehem?"
                                        Frances Chesterton.

Pages 47–48 Proverbs 20:27; Psalms 18:28; Isaiah 60:1; John 12:35, 36; I John 1:7; Psalms 4:6.

Page 49   From "Lead, Kindly Light,"
                                     John Henry Newman.

Page 87   From "The Retreate," Henry Vaughan.